KT-379-846

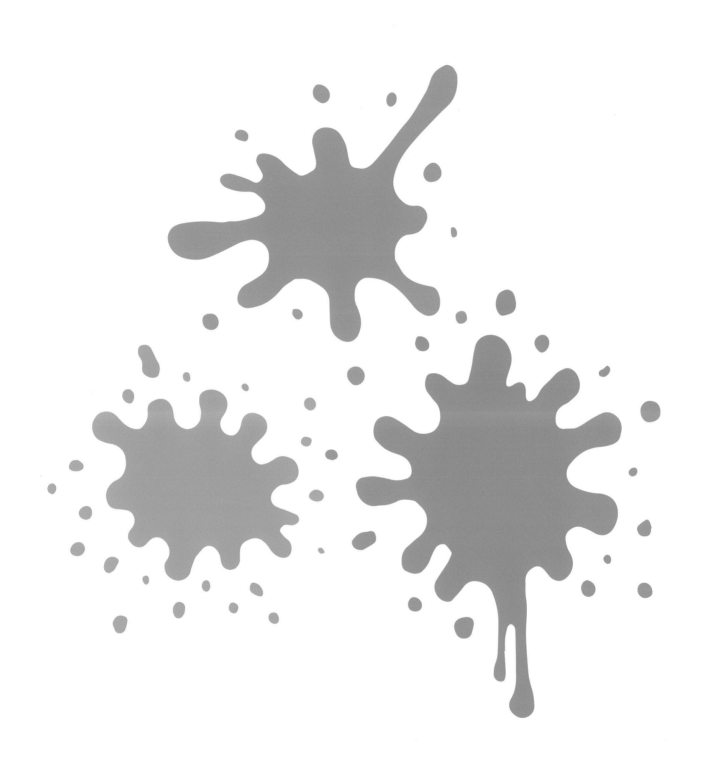

This book belongs to:

For Margot,
Delilah,
Mabel, Coco,
Augie and Oki.

Farshore

First published in Great Britain 2023 by Farshore
An imprint of HarperCollins*Publishers*
1 London Bridge Street, London SE1 9GF
www.farshore.co.uk

HarperCollins*Publishers*
Macken House, 39/40 Mayor Street Upper,
Dublin 1 D01 C9W8

Text and illustrations copyright © Matt Carr 2023
Matt Carr has asserted his moral rights.

ISBN 978 1 4052 9933 6
Printed in the UK by Bell and Bain Ltd, Glasgow.
001

A CIP catalogue record for this title is available from the British Library.

All rights reserved. No part of this publication may be reproduced,
stored in a retrieval system, or transmitted, in any form or by any
means, electronic, mechanical, photocopying, recording or otherwise,
without the prior permission of the publisher and copyright owner.

Stay safe online. Any website addresses listed in this book are correct
at the time of going to print. However, Farshore is not responsible for
content hosted by third parties. Please be aware that online content
can be subject to change and websites can contain content that is
unsuitable for children. We advise that all children are supervised
when using the internet.

Farshore takes its responsibility to the planet and its inhabitants
very seriously. We aim to use papers from well-managed forests
run by responsible suppliers.

Matt Carr

CAPTAIN LOOROLL

Farshore

Long ago, well probably around last Tuesday, an unlikely hero was born,
made from a magical talking tree called **THE EVERLASTING OAK.**

"You're super strong and endlessly long,
You can wipe up trouble when things go wrong.
You are more than just tissue – you have **HEART,** you have **SOUL.**

From this day forth you are . . .

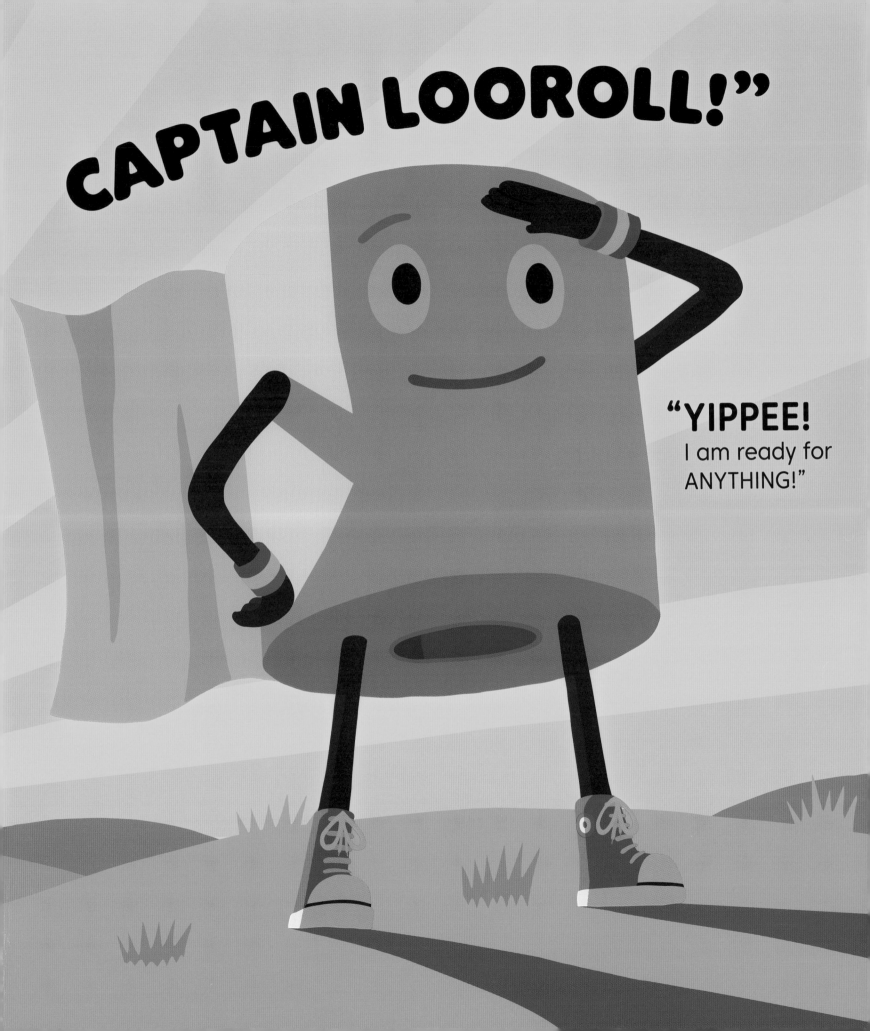

The only trouble was, in the toilet under the stairs, where Captain Looroll ended up, there wasn't **ANYTHING** to do. (Apart from wipe the odd bottom, which is not very heroic and not much fun.)

"I'm fed up hanging about all day," said Captain Looroll to her friends, Ray the Spray, Victoria Sponge and Barbara Bogbrush.

We need a bit of adventure.

"Don't worry, Captain. Something's bound to happen. **I can feel it in my water,**" said Victoria.

"You say that every day, Vic!" chuckled Ray.

But today Victoria was right. Something DID happen! An emergency call came down the pipe from the upstairs bathroom.

Calling CAPTAIN LOOROLL! Calling CAPTAIN LOOROLL! PLEASE COME QUICK. There's trouble in the toilet!

YIKES!

"At last, a proper mission!" cried Captain Looroll.
"Come on, Clean Team! **We need to get to the BOTTOM of this!**"

Using Captain Looroll's
SUPER STRENGTH,
they eventually made it
to the **TOP** of the stairs . . .

. . . and into the bathroom where
something **STRANGE** and **SLIMY**
was swirling around in the toilet.

Barbara's cousin, Barry, was very upset.

It's too much for my brush and it just won't flush!

What on earth
was going on?

Suddenly, something **PUNGENTLY PONGY**
leapt out and landed on the seat with a **SPLAT.**

"That is a ridiculously ambitious plan!" said the Captain. **"You won't get away with it, ToileTROLL!"**

"Oh, won't I?" sneered ToiletTROLL, leaping off the loo.

The friends followed a trail of funky footprints which led straight to the shower. "Looks like we've got him cornered, Captain," said Ray.

But when they pulled back the curtain . . .

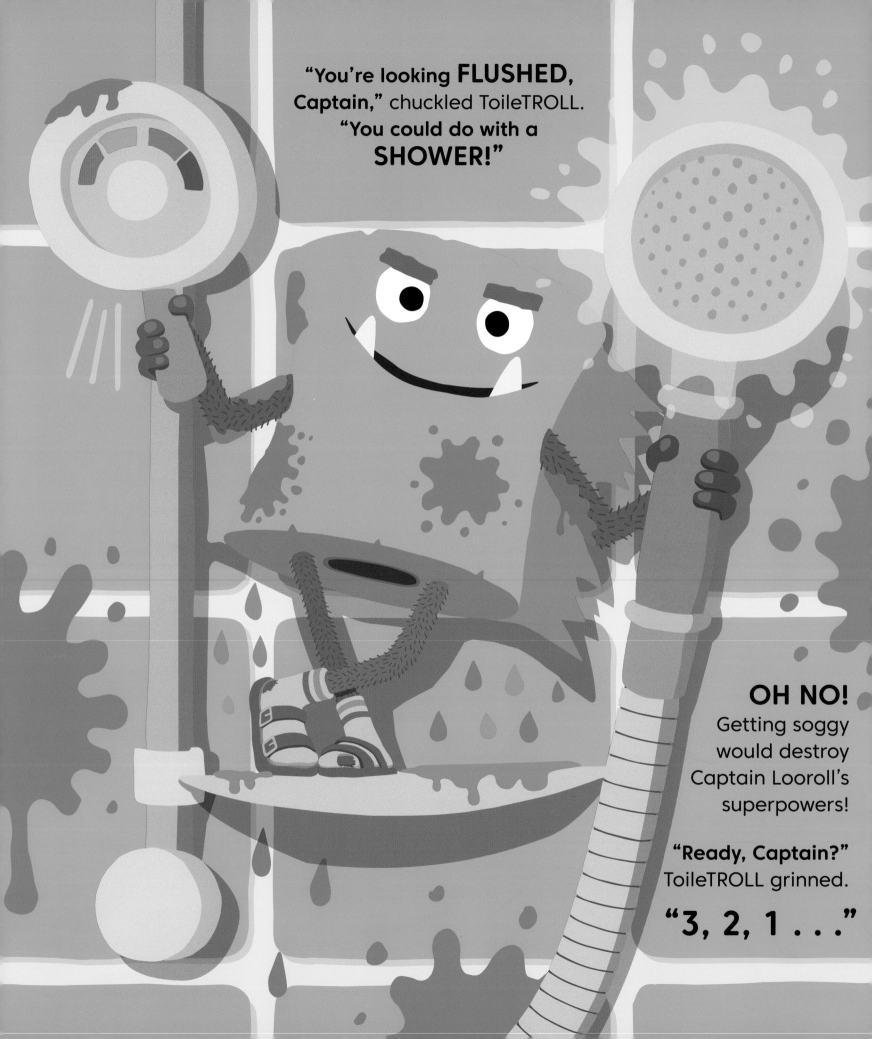

But it was **TOO LATE!**

"Look what he's done to the kids' bedroom!" gasped Ray.

YIPPEE!

BOING! BOING!

To be honest, it's not much worse than it usually is!

In a foul flash, ToileTROLL bounced away again.

See you later, Captain LOO-ser!

BUMP! BUMP! BUMP!

Hee-hee! This is fun!

A stream of messy missiles was flying straight towards them.

POW!
POW!
POW!

"Who wants some POOP-corn?" giggled ToileTROLL.

"Leave this to me, Captain," yelled Barbara . . .

WHACK!

. . . and she hit ToileTROLL for six!

Take that, you reeky rotter!

The mucky mayhem was far from over. **ToileTROLL had reached the fridge!**

Suddenly the Captain and her friends were engulfed in a bilious belch.

BURP!

COUGH!

SPLUTTER!

WHEEZE!

By the time Ray came to the rescue . . .

. . . **ToileTROLL was gone!**

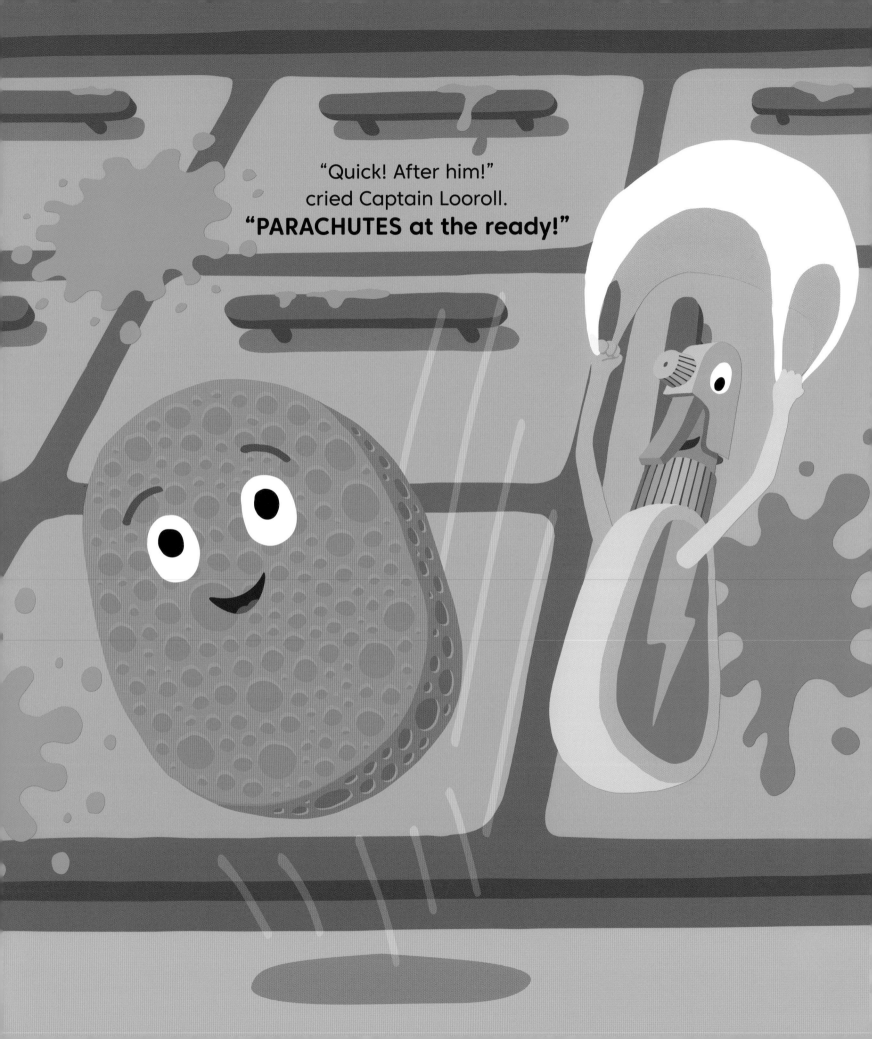

"Don't you mean **para-TISSUE-tes?**" giggled Vic, as they floated to the floor.

But before Captain Looroll could find ToileTROLL . . .

ToileTROLL found HER
(with the help of Dudley, the family pooch).

**"Hee-hee! You're going
to be in the dog house!"**
ToileTROLL cackled.

Now, Dudley just loved to play chase
as Captain Looroll was about to find out . . .

But ToileTROLL was so **SLIMY**, he slipped out of her lasso.

"Not so fast!" cried Captain Looroll. She made a grab for her naughty nemesis . . .

. . . and put the stinker in a **SPIN!**

Oh bother!